Piglet Tells the Truth

written by Dr. Mary Manz Simon
illustrated by Dorothy Stott

09 08 07 06 05 04 03   9 8 7 6 5 4 3 2 1

Standard
PUBLISHING

CINCINNATI, OHIO

www.standardpub.com

Piglet, Piglet,
share today,
what the Bible
has to say...

When I say
I will be true,
that means
I won't lie to you.

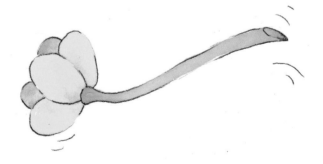

If I make
a great big mess,
I'll be honest
and confess.

I will not steal
from a store.
I will pay
at the front door.

I will keep
my promise true.
That is being
honest, too.

If I say,
"I'll clean my room,"
I will use
a mop and broom.

When God tells me,
"I love you,"
those three words
are honest, too.

Oink, oink!
I will say and do
What I think
and know is true.

Know what's false and what is true. What does honest mean to you?

"I have chosen the way of truth."
Psalm 119:30